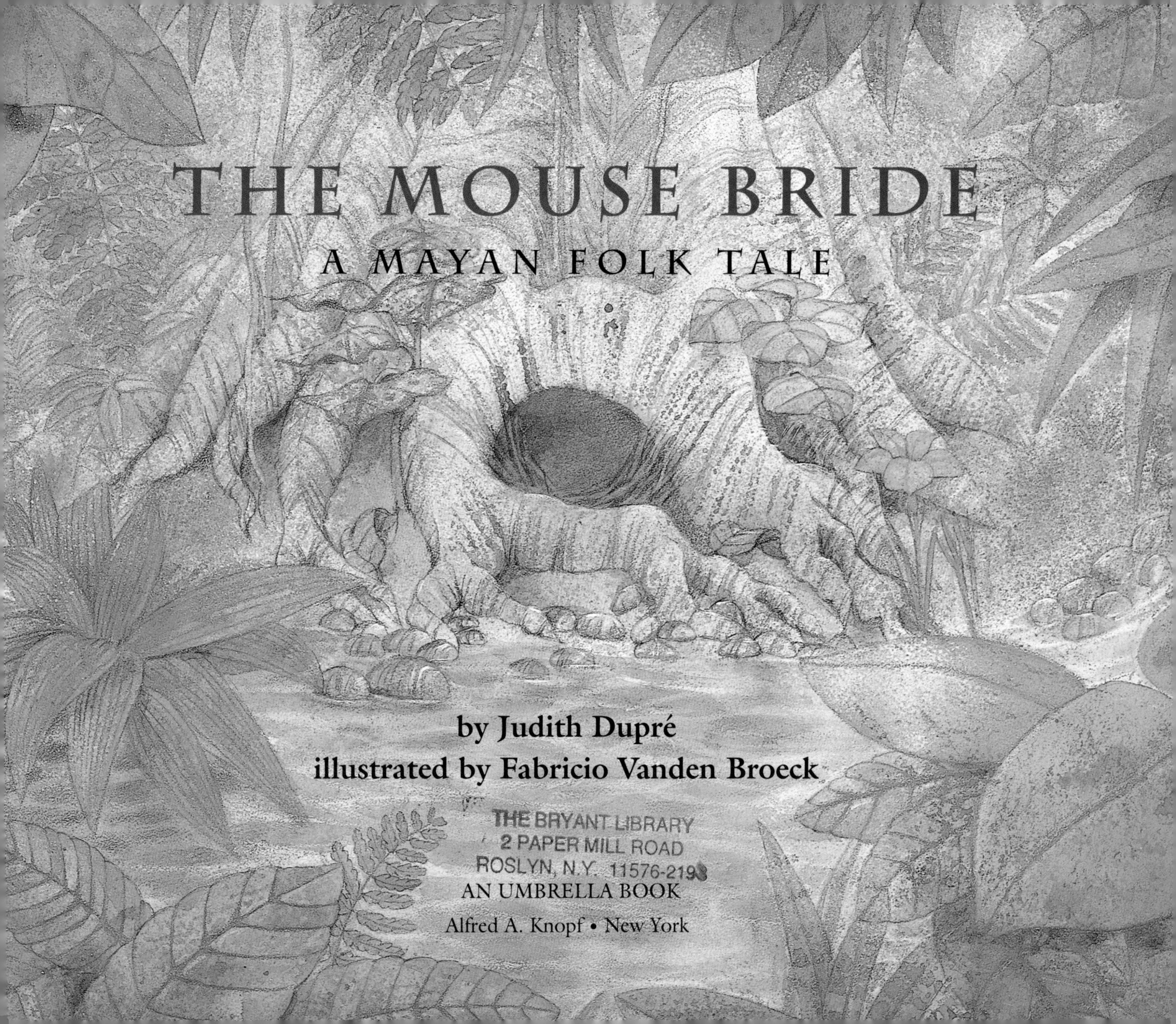

THE MOUSE BRIDE

A MAYAN FOLK TALE

by Judith Dupré

illustrated by Fabricio Vanden Broeck

AN UMBRELLA BOOK

Alfred A. Knopf • New York

AN UMBRELLA BOOK PUBLISHED BY ALFRED A. KNOPF, INC.

Text copyright © 1993 by Judith Dupré
Illustrations copyright © 1993 by Fabricio Vanden Broeck

Library of Congress Cataloging-in-Publication Data

Dupré, Judith.
The mouse bride / by Judith Dupré ; illustrated by Fabricio Vanden Broeck.
Summary: A mother and father mouse search for the perfect husband for their beautiful daughter.
ISBN 0-679-83273-4 (trade) — ISBN 0-679-93273-9 (lib. bdg.)
1. Chol Indians — Legends. 2. Mayas — Legends. [1. Chol Indians — Legends.
2. Indians of Mexico — Legends. 3. Mayas — Legends.]
I. Broeck, Fabricio Vanden, 1954–   ill. II. Title. III. Series. F1221.C57D86   1993
398.2'0972 — dc20   [E]   92-15275

Manufactured in the United States of America

2   4   6   8   0   9   7   5   3   1

For my sisters, Cindy and Susan

— J. D.

For Nadia, Carlo, and Fabio

— F. V. B.

There once were two mice who had the most beautiful little daughter. Not a day went by that they did not marvel at her perfection.

"Look at her pink nose, my love. Is it not more delicate than the roses that bloom?

"Look at her eyes, which glisten like the round brown stones in the brook.

"Her fur is as soft as the light in early morning," they said as they stroked their precious one. "She has wrapped us around her heart.

"Her feet are tiny and strong. All four will take her far."

The thought of their daughter going into the world with its many dark corners made the father mouse and the mother mouse tremble so hard that the dew fell from the flowers above.

That night the two mice made a plan.
"We shall find the perfect husband for our beautiful daughter, one as noble and good as she, so she will always have a companion by her side."

When the Moon came over the horizon, the two mice asked her for advice. "Tell us, who is the most powerful in the universe, for we have a beautiful daughter for him to marry."

And the Moon said, "Why, the Sun, of course. Every morning he chases me from the sky and then shines so that all of life might grow. The Sun is surely the most powerful."

The mouse parents decided they would ask the Sun to marry their daughter.
The next morning they wrapped her in a fern and went to the Sun and said,

"Sun, we would like you to marry our daughter."

"Why should I?" asked the Sun.

"Because she is perfect in every way. Her nose is as pink as a rose, her eyes
glisten like the stones in a brook, and in her paws she holds the universe.
You are the most powerful, so you should be her groom."

"But I am not the most powerful," said the Sun. "When the Cloud fills the
sky, he blocks my light. The Cloud is the most powerful, so he should marry
your daughter."

Before long, the Cloud floated by. When the mouse parents asked him to marry their daughter, he laughed until teardrops ran down his cheeks and he said,

"Yes, I block the light of the Sun that hides the Moon, but when the Wind blows, he chases me away. The Wind is the most powerful, so he should marry your daughter."

The grass rustled. The leaves began to sing. It was the Wind. Wrapping the fern tightly around their little one, the mice turned to face him.

"Why are you here?" howled the huge and fearsome Wind.

The mice clung to a clover stem to keep from blowing away.

"He *must* be the most powerful one in the universe," whispered Mrs. Mouse.

"What did you say?" roared the Wind.

"Well, sir, we want you to marry our perfect baby daughter, because you are the most powerful in the universe and can protect her from the dark corners of the world," said the father mouse. He gently lifted the fern covering the mouse bride so the Wind could see her perfection for himself.

"But I am not the most powerful," said the Wind. "Why, I am easily stopped by a wall." He drew a deep breath and flung it against a stone wall. The Wall didn't budge.

"The Wall is much stronger than me. The Sun is blocked by the Cloud that is chased by the Wind that is stopped by the Wall.

"It is clear to me your daughter should marry a wall."

And so the mouse family took their tiny daughter to the Wall. Seeing its great height and width, they shouted, in a shy way,

"Will you marry our daughter? She is perfect in every way and should go into the world with someone by her side. The Sun said the Cloud was more powerful than he, and the Cloud said the Wind was more powerful than he, and the Wind said you were more powerful than he," and so they shouted, in a shy way,

"Will you marry our daughter?"

"Well," said the Wall, "it is true I stop the Wind that chases the Cloud that blocks the Sun. But my dear mice, there's someone much more powerful than me. Though I am very tall and stretch as far as you can see, I crumble when a mouse burrows through me. A mouse is the most powerful. Therefore your daughter should marry a mouse."

The father mouse and the mother mouse looked at each other and smiled.

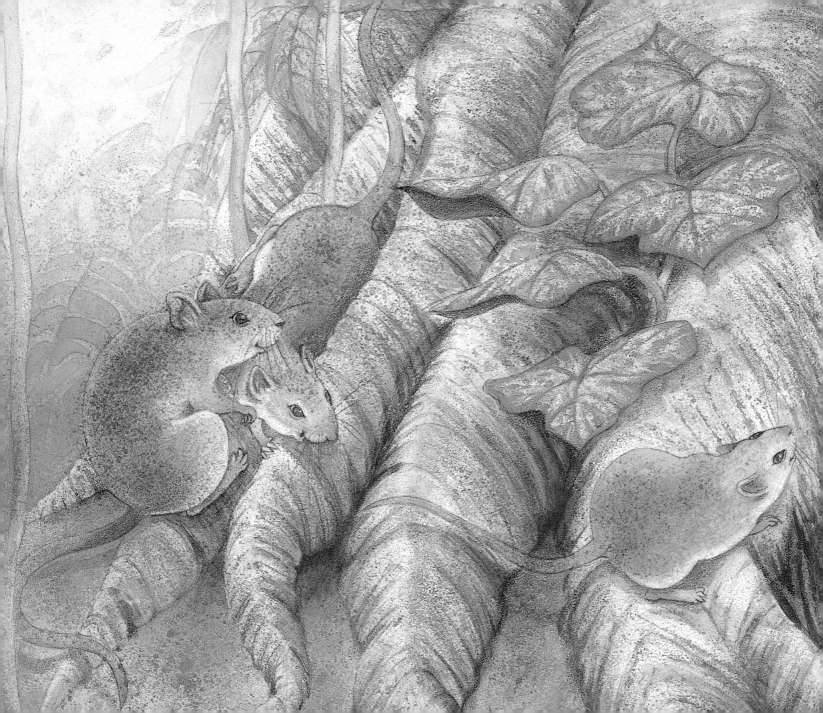

When they returned home, a perfect
mouse groom was waiting for them.

The mother mouse wove a veil of spider webs. The father mouse gathered fruit and grains from all the neighborhood homes. The mouse groom searched the sky for the perfect star for his perfect bride.

At last the wedding day came.

The Moon beamed.

The Sun shone.

The Cloud cried tears of joy, but just a few.

The Wind cooled the mice as they danced round and round.

And the Wall contained all the joy of their meeting.

The father mouse and the mother mouse thanked the Moon for helping them find the perfect groom for their perfect daughter, and went to bed.

A NOTE FROM THE AUTHOR

This story is based on a fable told by the Chol Indians, who live in the rainforest of Chiapas, a state in Mexico. Most Chols live in a village near Palenque, the ancient home of their Mayan ancestors. Palenque is a city of magnificent palaces and stepped temples covered with hieroglyphics, a type of picture language carved in stone. It was built over a thousand years ago deep in the heart of the overgrown jungle. The endpapers in this book were inspired by hieroglyphics found on the Temple of the Sun and the Temple of the Cross, whose ruins still stand in Palenque.

Many stories are told by the Chols to explain their beautiful, though unpredictable, environment — one where the rainy season lasts nine months! It's not surprising to learn that when the Chols speak, their words sound like the rain hitting rock and reflect their love of music and sense of play. They do not have a written language.

While visiting the ruins at Palenque, I met an elderly Chol Indian who is one of the few in the village to speak English. He told me the story of the mouse bride. This myth is told and retold to each generation of children so that they might understand the circular ways of Nature and make peace with the harsh sun and torrential rains of their home.